PRA

5⁻1ᴦ

Tom Clancy fans open to a strong female lead will clamor for more.

— *DRONE*, PUBLISHERS WEEKLY

Superb!

— *DRONE*, BOOKLIST STARRED REVIEW

The best military thriller I've read in a very long time. Love the female characters.

— *DRONE*, SHELDON MCARTHUR, FOUNDER OF THE MYSTERY BOOKSTORE, LA

A fabulous soaring thriller.

— *TAKE OVER AT MIDNIGHT*, MIDWEST BOOK REVIEW

Meticulously researched, hard-hitting, and suspenseful.

— *PURE HEAT*, PUBLISHERS WEEKLY, STARRED REVIEW

Expert technical details abound, as do realistic military missions with superb imagery that will have readers feeling as if they are right there in the midst and on the edges of their seats.

— *LIGHT UP THE NIGHT,* RT REVIEWS, 4 1/2 STARS

Buchman has catapulted his way to the top tier of my favorite authors.

— FRESH FICTION

Nonstop action that will keep readers on the edge of their seats.

— *TAKE OVER AT MIDNIGHT,* LIBRARY JOURNAL

M L. Buchman's ability to keep the reader right in the middle of the action is amazing.

— LONG AND SHORT REVIEWS

The only thing you'll ask yourself is, "When does the next one come out?"

— *WAIT UNTIL MIDNIGHT,* RT REVIEWS, 4 STARS

The first...of (a) stellar, long-running (military) romantic suspense series.

— *THE NIGHT IS MINE,* BOOKLIST, "THE 20 BEST ROMANTIC SUSPENSE NOVELS: MODERN MASTERPIECES"

I knew the books would be good, but I didn't realize how good.

— NIGHT STALKERS SERIES, KIRKUS REVIEWS

Buchman mixes adrenalin-spiking battles and brusque military jargon with a sensitive approach.

— PUBLISHERS WEEKLY

13 times "Top Pick of the Month"

— NIGHT OWL REVIEWS

TEAM BLACK SHEEP

5-12-20

A NIGHT STALKER CSAR MILITARY ROMANCE

M. L. BUCHMAN

Buchman Bookworks

SIGN UP FOR M. L. BUCHMAN'S NEWSLETTER TODAY

and receive:
Release News
Free Short Stories
a Free Book

Get your free book today. Do it now.
free-book.mlbuchman.com

Other works by M. L. Buchman:

Short Story Series by M. L. Buchman:

ABOUT THIS BOOK

The most dangerous mission of all: CSAR—Combat Search and Rescue.

__Sergeant Gerrard "Doc" Carson's__ main claim to fame? Being the black sheep of his family. His solution to sign up as an Army grunt? About to cost him and his sharpshooter teammate Smith, and cost them bad. Hunkered down in Niger's capital city during a coupe, his squad's future is headed for that seriously permanent kind of Army discharge.

When __Medic Teri Carson__ and a full flight of the 160th Night Stalkers come to the rescue, he gets a new appreciation for the CSAR mission. But when "Doc" finds out Teri also holds the title of Black Sheep, he knows he's onto something special.

TIMING

THIS TITLE OCCURS THREE YEARS PRIOR TO THE EVENTS IN *Night Stalkers* #2, I Own the Dawn.

1

February 10th, 2010
Niamey, Niger, Central Africa

"Okay, there are probably worse places to die. But please don't tell me about them."

"Deal," Smith offered one of her typically verbose responses, then glanced at her watch.

Gerrard Carson tried to resist, but couldn't, and checked his own watch as he frantically applied another bandage. He wasn't even looking at whose limb it was anymore.

Nine of them with their backs against a building. A low adobe-brick wall to their left and their flipped and shattered pickup truck angled across the rest of the opening. Triage was long gone out the window—except their truck no longer had windows.

Graveyard humor. The God-given right of every Army grunt about to go down hard. *Hooah!*

He saw blood and did his best to staunch it. That was all he could do in the short time. A streaming scalp wound through blond hair? Yeah, he knew who that was but didn't have time to think of their name.

The prayer call from the minaret of the local mosque had been going on for three minutes and thirty seconds. It was Asr in the capital city of Niger—when the length of his afternoon shadow matched his own height, and everyone in Niamey stopped to pray.

A strange hiatus in the midst of a pitched battle.

Max of ninety seconds left before prayer ended and the battle resumed. And that's only if they were lucky and the attackers took the full five minutes to thank God for the chance to kill their team.

Officially only a hundred and nine degrees today, the hottest major city in the world felt like one-twenty and rising fast.

"We're cookin' here." Of course that could also be because the south-facing wall at their backs was the burnt-orange-dulled-under-brown-dust front of the corporate offices for fat-cat-people-he-didn't-give-a-damn-about. American contractors in the middle of Niamey—not the military type, the money type.

"Meat," Smith offered the ultimate insult to an infantryman. *Meat.* Not worth anything else. Just part of the military machine.

About right.

They were being cooked and chewed up. Not that many more minutes until they'd be spit out for good, but he had to try. He unsnapped a rifle sling, and tied it around someone's thigh. He slid an empty twenty-round magazine through it as a turning stick and spun it tight. At least the leg stopped pumping blood. Grabbing the soldier's hand, he put it on the jury-rigged tourniquet and shouted in his face, "Do *not* let go of this."

He didn't wait for any acknowledgement, or let himself focus to see who it was. Just let go of the guy's hand on the magazine and hoped for the best.

They'd been in the city doing training with the Presidential guards. Until suddenly Nigerien President Tandja was getting his ass coup d'étated.

"Coup is probably over," Smith scanned outside their hide between a low wall and the chassis of their flipped pickup truck. "Not that we'll ever know."

Also right.

Their staff sergeant had done good. He'd extricated his eight shooters from the situation as it wasn't an American battle. Once clear of the battle at the Presidential palace, they were tasked to set up protection on a cluster of offices used by US corporations in case the whole city went bad. He'd pulled it off, and they'd fallen all the way back clean.

Should have been fine. Back street several blocks back from the palace.

Except some Nigerien yay-hoo had decided that the American team were actually escaping Presidential guards.

Just as they'd pulled up at what was supposed to be a quiet guard detail, someone had RPG'd their pickup—probably shouldn't have lifted it from the President's guards when they'd needed to be gone fast.

Real useful thought in hindsight.

Then they'd offered the staff sergeant a bullet to his brainpan before anyone could even blink—which put them down to eight and no leader between one heartbeat and the next.

Smith had taken out the shooter—just too late for the staff sergeant. She was so damned good that it was like having a real countersniper, which would never happen in an eight-grunt squad. He'd set his M4 carbine to three-rounds burst and counted himself lucky if he got a hit. She fired semi-auto singles and never missed.

"Thirty seconds, Doc," Smith saved him checking his watch again.

That actually gave him a moment's pause. Usually he was "Low Gear" because apparently Gerrard was too complex a name for most grunts. He'd rather be "High Gear" but a grunt never got any say in his tag. He'd always been the steady one in the squad, so maybe Low Gear fit.

But "Doc"?

He was simply the guy who still remembered his dinnertime training. Mom was an operating room nurse and Dad an ER doc. Even his big sister was interning by the time he graduated high school. Dinner conversations were predictably bloody. When he'd gone grunt instead of med school—major parental disappointment—he'd been the one guy wholly unabashed by blood and guts. It was also the best way he'd been able to think of for escaping family peer pressure. Five years on? He was thinking going Army grunt rather than college was a pretty dumb-ass idea.

He could wrap a bandage with the best of them, but

that was all. He was just a gun on a squad, and nowhere near the kind of shooter that Smith was. Not that either skill meant a whole lot at the moment. They weren't a big enough team to warrant a trained EMT, and Niamey was a peaceful place—until today. They needed a whole team of top shooters even more than the medico.

The squad was getting pretty light on the ground. Two were past lifting their weapons—ever again. A glance showed that the tourniquet had slid loose from a grip gone lax, and so they were down a third. Three others were still in it only because they weren't going to the big discharge in the sky without a fight. And the staff sergeant was long past caring about that bullet in the brainpan.

That left him and Smith as the only fully able shooters.

Tags never stuck to Smith. She was just...Smith. She'd been knocked back in rank a couple times—no one knew why—but Sergeant Smith was a hell-bitch in a firefight.

At four minutes-fifty after the call to five minutes of prayer had begun, he grabbed his rifle to protect what was left of his squad.

The dusty street looked impossibly serene. Ten meters wide and about five blocks long in either direction before it jogged or twisted out of sight among the one- and two-story structures.

Pale red-brown sand. Buildings in a dozen shades of beige because the dust and sand washed out all colors.

"I'm gonna die in beige."

"No," Smith blew the dust off her scope. Kicked up by every muzzle blast, the stuff just hung in the air until it found some optics to blur. "We're gonna die bright red."

Gerrard carefully didn't look behind him at the seeping bandages he'd managed to put on the remainder of the team.

2

NOTHING WAS IN THE RIGHT PLACE.

On her own bird, Teri knew right where everything was.

But this wasn't a Night Stalkers flight, it was a USAF flight—surrounded by US Army Night Stalkers.

Air Force medics must be part Alaskan king crab with arms twice as long as any normal human. The bandages and the surgical kit were on opposite sides of the Pave Hawk's bay, at least two meters apart. And the drugs were nowhere near the plasma cooler which wasn't where she found the IV gear at all. Maybe they were octopi.

She liked that image. If she thought like an octopod, the layout almost made sense. Or like medics who usually flew in pairs. But that was a much less fun image.

Once again, her life was all disjointed.

Typically the Night Stalkers was just the opposite. She'd always liked structure, being able to see everything in a single gestalt. She'd liked it as a little kid, and the Army had offered that in spades. Special Operations times ten. There was a constant striving for the best, the most efficient, the most effective. A honing inward until everything was a perfect rote action.

Being a medic offered the same. Step One, Step Two, Step Three. In battle medicine, every moment or symptom became a logical decision-branch of choices. Breathing? Blood: spurting, flowing, or trickling...

The missions themselves, even the ones without a lengthy briefing, were still highly predictable for her life as a combat medic.

Fly into the zone three minutes behind the warfighters.

Lurk outside the zone.

Someone got hit or went down? Head in full tilt no matter what shitstorm was brewing.

By end of mission no one hit? Fly back just as clean and quiet as they'd arrived.

But not this time.

"One minute out," the pilot announced.

"Thanks." It was their longest conversation yet, which fit her down to the bones.

She peeked out the window. A mud brown river was wide and lazy here, like sluggish blood flowing through the heart of the typical African city. A handful or so of eight- to ten-story buildings scattered through a sprawling city of dusty streets and low adobe and concrete structures.

Teri preferred to focus inside the helo. *This* world she knew and understood.

Except here her gestalt was fractured into fifty pieces, like looking at someone with one eye where their nose should be and the other in their ear. With their lips out the back of their head, and their nose sniffing the sky so that you couldn't help but see right up the nostrils and...

It was the same as every time she looked at her brother's art. He was in what critics had dubbed his "Picasso phase", not that she could tell it from anything else. It made even less sense to her than when Picasso had done it, but then she'd never understood her brother, never mind his art.

Or her parents' art.

She'd been the odd one, the "scientist" in the artistic family.

That's what they always called her: Ms. Science. It had almost followed her into the military. But by keeping her mouth shut and her head down, others generally left her out of their conversations. Just the way she liked it.

Now, once again, her "odd choices" were leading her to even odder places.

This mission had been scrambled off their ship, the USS *Peleliu* in the Gulf of Guinea, at the first news of the coup in Niger. Except the Night Stalkers had already sent their transports on a goodwill training mission to Senegal —so there was no combat search-and-rescue bird for her.

Without a CSAR flight, she'd grabbed sixty pounds of medical bag and tucked herself into a corner of the DAP Hawk gunship between a SEAL Team 6 commander and a four-thousand-round ammo case for one of the Miniguns.

Being resourceful, the Night Stalkers had picked up a flight of US Air Force Pave Hawks that had been visiting Ghana—four transports and two medical evac birds—

but they'd only had one medic thanks to some awful bug
one of the guys had picked up in the night market.

So, they'd refueled in northern Ghana and switched
her over to the strange world of the Pave Hawk Alaskan
crab kings. She'd meant to look at the other medic to see
if his arms were normal-sized, but missed her chance.

3

"Doc! Last full mag!" Someone—Jethro? Yes, by the bloody head bandage over his blond hair—hit the release dropping his rifle magazine into the dirt. Unable to move enough to shoot anymore, he flapped a hand to offer it.

Looked like "Doc" was going to be his new tag—for the last few minutes of his life. Fine, he'd own that. Time to deal out some 5.56 mm medicine.

He turned and saw blood streaming down Smith's waist. She was still kneeling at the edge of their hole and firing.

Shit! If Smith went down, he was definitely toast.

A bullet must have skipped off a wall, ducked behind the pickup, and gone through-and-through just below her ribs. While grabbing the mag, it must have missed his head by inches. He'd certainly never heard it go by.

He yanked off his gear belt, slapped it around her middle, and cinched it tight.

Not one damn word. Not even a grunt of pain.

Doc wondered for the hundredth time what drove her. It was a question that no one asked twice. Anyone who asked got the "Look" that said death was coming for them if they were shit-stupid enough to ask again. He counted himself smart because he'd never actually asked even once.

He rapped the salvaged mag on his helmet to seat all the rounds to the rear of the carrier, and slapped it into his own rifle. He flipped the selector to semi-auto—against his better judgement—to conserve the last of their ammo, and yanked the charging handle to load a round in the chamber.

Coming up out of the hole ready to fire the moment his scope lined up, he didn't lack for targets.

But even as he lined up, he knew he was too late.

Someone had anticipated where he'd be popping up.

Time slowed.

There was a distinctive look to a rifle aimed in your general direction versus one that was dead on. Was that how Smith operated? Every shot finding that perfect alignment where the target was no longer a question but now a certainty.

No time—he fired.

Even as he did, he knew it was his usual six- or seven-ring shot, not the ten-point bullseye that he needed.

For a full point-seven seconds that his round was traveling the fifty meters, he knew he was looking straight into death's maw. He would never move fast enough to get clear of the return fire.

Then, through his scope, he saw the target blown backward.

Shredded.

The man's rifle tossed upward in reaction to the hit.

No way did a NATO 5.56 mm round do that on impact.

Then Doc heard the buzzsaw.

Emerging over a low building, a pitch-black Black Hawk helicopter slid into view. Lead was pouring out in three directions. Not only were both of the crew chiefs' side-mounted Miniguns slicing into the attackers, but the hard-mounted forward gun as well.

Smith grabbed his collar and jerked him down out of view.

She grunted as he landed hard against her.

"Sorry."

"Just keep your damn head down. That's a 160th Night Stalkers DAP Hawk and it cuts a wide swath."

The buzzsaw cut off after just another three seconds, leaving only the pounding thud of the blades washing down from the sky and rattling between the buildings.

There was a moment with no other fire. From anyone.

"Damn, but that's precision." Smith was looking up at the sky. "Night Stalkers rock."

He peeked up in time to see four Little Bird helos arriving from the four points of the compass. Simultaneously, they all slid to a halt like goddamned synchronized swimmers.

Fire resumed from their attackers, now directed at the helos in the sky.

Spec Ops of some sort started roping down from where they'd been sitting on the side-mounted bench seats—four per bird. Those above providing cover fire to those heading down. As each reached the ground, he knelt, shouldered his rifle, and began taking out additional targets. Semi-auto, single-round shots Doc noted with some chagrin.

"I want to cry, I'm so happy." He spotted a rifle slipping out of a window down the block.

He fired too fast and his round skipped off the lower sill.

Smith nailed the shooter, and he tumbled back into the darkness.

"We might just get out of this."

"Chickens," she said as she popped up and fired another round at the window without appearing to even look first.

He peeked out to see that, sure enough, another shooter had come to the window—probably with the dead man's weapon. No, *definitely* with the dead man's weapon. Smith had simply known how long it would take someone to grab it from the dead man and return to the window.

"Okay, still eggs." He wasn't going to start counting his chickens until he was somewhere hell-and-gone away from here.

It was his first major firefight. He hoped to God it was going to be his last. He'd somehow avoided the grinder of Iraq and Afghanistan, mostly pulling base duty in one place or another.

Maybe he'd just stay hunkered down right here.

"Hey there." A deep voice sounded from above him. He looked up at the helmeted American looking at him over the shattered engine of the pickup truck. "Y'all want a ride?"

Okay, maybe it was okay to count to "one"—even while he was still an egg.

4

TERI PAID NO ATTENTION TO THE UNHARMED CORPORATE types streaming out of the office building and onto the big Pave Hawk transports which had landed in the street intersection.

They loaded her bird with five soldiers in a bay rated for two litters. Four more went to the other bird; no longer her problem.

No second medic—her choices were limited.

Soldier One?

No pulse. No blood pressure. Oxygenation low to near zero.

Bad signs.

Temperature actually significantly higher than normal.

That gave her pause.

But only for a moment.

The outdoor temperature here was significantly higher than body temperature. And the sudden transition from the full heat of battle to a stopped heart, meant that the body was no longer able to cool itself by circulating blood and producing sweat.

This body's core was superheated to 109.

She'd need ice packs, shock paddles, units of whole blood, and time.

Teri had everything but the last.

Moving on.

Soldier Two had the three-chevrons-and-a-rocker insignia of a staff sergeant—and a large hole where his brain was supposed to be.

She rolled him on top of the other one to make some room. They were past caring and she certainly didn't.

With a quick glance she assessed the other three soldiers.

One appeared to be mobile.

One critical.

The third, a woman, her dusky skin pale, still sat upright in the cargo bay doorway, her rifle tracking below as they lifted. There was a wide, dark blood stain on her back.

"You," she shouted at the mobile one.

"Doc."

"Fine. Doc. Get some pressure on those wounds," she pointed at the woman. "Then get her stitched up."

Teri then turned to the other victim and began her triage inspection.

5

Doc? He'd actually introduced himself to a real *medic* as Doc? He was about the furthest thing there could be from that.

The woman had hands like nitrile-blue lightning. Between one eyeblink and the next, she'd inspected the grunt—Jethro now out cold with his head bandage dark red—rolled him on his left side for a blood check, then eased him onto his back. All of his wounds were up front —a man who faced the enemy. Too bad he'd faced them for so long.

Two hundred meters up, the Pave Hawks—filled with the "corporates" he'd nearly died defending but had never even seen—turned for the airport. Get them on a jet and get them home.

But their own bird and another just like it, surrounded by a cluster of black helicopters, turned south for the coast.

He glanced at Smith just in time to grab her as she

slumped. A moment later and she'd have rolled forward out the cargo door nose-first and gone for a swim in the Niger River along with the West African crocodiles. Even Smith probably couldn't take them on.

He hauled her the rest of the way into the cramped cargo bay and laid her on her back.

"Blood type?" the female medic called out.

He checked Smith's dog tag, "Type A positive."

"Good. I've got some of that. Here," she tossed over a squishy plastic bag of dark red blood. "Get her tapped and get that into her. Then close those wounds."

"Tapped?" He asked, just as a small plastic bag smacked him in the chest. It had a needle in it, like he was supposed to know what to do with that. "How—"

"No time. I've got to save this one."

"Jethro."

"I'm Teri," she said without looking up.

"No. He's Jethro. I'm Gerrard 'Low Gear' 'Doc' Carson."

She was one cut from completely slicing off Jethro's shirt—no bullet-proof vests because they'd just been on a friendly training assignment in a non-combative country. She stopped and looked directly at him for the first time. Her face was narrow and fine-featured, a slip of blonde hair poked out of her helmet—and her gaze a laser-intent blue almost as bright as her gloves.

"What?" Doc looked down to see if he was suddenly bleeding without knowing it.

"Carson?"

"Yes, of the incredibly not famous Boston General medical Carsons. Why?"

"Teri *Carson*. Of the Alaskan Carsons. Now get her tapped and sealed up, Doc," she nodded to Smith then refocused on Jethro. The more clothing she cut away, the more blood there was to see. It was going to take a miracle to get him home.

"Doc" felt pretty damn stupid as a tag at the moment.

One more glance at Teri as she rolled out a surgical kit with a practiced snap.

Gerrard was looking for gloves when a pair of nitriles smacked him in the face.

Teri was looking down, but she might have been smiling.

He pulled them on—plenty around their house to play with as a kid—and rolled up Smith's sleeve. Opening the packet for the tap needle he was ready with everything except how to do it.

"Teri?" If she heard him, she didn't look up. She had a pair of long-nose forceps plunged deep into Jethro's shoulder. Even as he watched, she pulled up a bullet which was followed by a fast flow of blood.

"Shit! Hurry up, Doc. I'm going to need you over here."

Doc looked down at Smith's exposed arm and the needle he was holding. There were iodine swabs in the packet.

He swabbed her arm for thirty long seconds just like when he donated blood. Then a second swab wipe.

No tracks. So drugs weren't unknown Smith's past.

Rather than asking for a tourniquet, he pinched the artery on the inside of Smith's upper arm—just as his mom had when he'd sliced his hand really badly once while slicing a bagel. The vein didn't exactly bulge in the crook of her elbow, but he could see it.

"Sorry about this, Smith."

Then he took a deep breath and jabbed the needle in.

6

Teri couldn't figure out Doc Carson.

He fumbled and looked panicked like he didn't know anything. Then he did the iodine by the book and knew the trick with pinching the brachial artery.

It was sweet the way he apologized to his girlfriend before he jabbed her with the needle. As if she wasn't way past feeling it.

Teri cut down deep enough to find the bleeder in Jethro's subclavian artery. A stapler and a little backup glue had it pasted back together. No time to deal with the little bleeders, she jammed in a surgical sponge and shifted to the next hole.

"Here." She tossed him a fresh package of sponges. "If your girlfriend isn't bleeding too much when you pull that strap, just shove this in."

"Not my girlfriend. We're fireteam leaders in the same squad is all."

"Why not? She's pretty." She had the full chest and serious curves that Carsons never developed.

"Because she's lethal as hell."

Maybe he was right. Even passed out cold and pale from blood loss she looked extremely determined.

Though in all that dark hair, Smith had a single streak of blonde as light as Teri's own hair. It softened her and added to her mystery.

"Get moving!" Teri said it as much for her own benefit as for Doc's.

Again that strange hesitation before he swung into action.

Then, working quickly, he released the gear belt, sliced open her blouse—about two whole inches.

"All the way up. Get the fabric out of the way."

"Damn good thing she's not awake, she'd kill me," he muttered as he continued the slice up to her collar and folded the shirt completely aside, fully exposing her sports bra.

More than necessary, but she didn't care. Instead Teri watched long enough to see that blood flowed, but didn't pump out. "Sprinkle in some antibiotic powder, and insert the sponge. Wrap her in gauze then get over here."

7

DOC DECIDED THAT IT WAS A GOOD THING THAT SMITH WAS out, otherwise she *would* kill him—because damn but the woman was built, and it was majorly tough not to stare. He also saw that it was far from her first wound. Knife scars on the abdomen and shoulder. Another deep gash, wide and high on the ribs, that might have been another bullet wound.

Or maybe a broadsword.

Whatever Smith had been through, it had been a world filled with lots of pain.

His own "big" scars to date were appendicitis, and a broken glass jar that had sliced his hand really badly once and needed five stitches when he was a kid. The bagel-slicing incident hadn't really left a scar.

He rapped knuckles against his helmet. Hopefully, that would be all—ever. No question but he was out of battle. He'd do anything he had to not to head up another fireteam.

One glance at the two bodies...corpses off to the side.

The staff sergeant and one of Smith's team. If Jethro made it, that would be at least one other from his squad.

"Why wasn't I hit?"

"So that you could get over here and help me."

He tied off the wrap around Smith, doublechecked that there weren't any other bloody spots on her, and then shifted over.

They worked over Jethro methodically. Plugging leaks and holes one by one.

He handed Teri instruments, hung another bag of plasma, mopped up blood from the deck, and became pretty handy with the flesh glue. The hours he'd spent building model airplanes kept him from gluing his gloves to any of Jethro's wounds.

"So, Teri of the Alaskan Carsons, what brought you here?"

"Black Hawk helicopter," her tone was so dry that she seemed to desiccate the spilled blood on the deck before he could wipe it away.

He laughed. "Wind back a bit more than that, Teri."

"Hold this." He grabbed the retractor to keep the wound open as she probed for another round.

"Shit, Jethro, dude. You gotta learn when to duck." Jethro was out, but the monitors said his heart was still ticking. Amazing with the number of holes in him.

"Family black sheep," she spoke as if nothing unusual was going on.

"Black sheep! Hooah!" He offered a high-five.

She looked at his bloody glove, rolled her eyes, but he was pretty sure that she was smiling under her mask.

It wasn't a round that she pulled out, but the truck's key that had somehow projectiled into his thigh.

"What was *your* failing?" It was clear that it was up to him to keep her talking.

"Not an artist." Teri was almost as voluble as Smith. "Family of artists," she doubled her word count.

"Doing a pretty damn fine job of putting Jethro back into one piece. ...Wait a sec." Doc squinted at her. "My sister is big on some Carson from Alaska. Has a painting, well, a print of a painting, of spring melt-out all gold and red with sunlight."

"She has taste. That's Mom's work."

"Holy shit. I'm here with someone famous."

"So not," Teri glared down at Jethro's body, but they'd run out of things to fix.

He'd been following along behind her, closing each of Jethro's wounds and taping gauze over the finished work. He'd also been doing the antiseptic and bandage thing on scrapes from shattered chunks of burnt-orange wall and the like.

"You look like a patchwork quilt, Jethro."

8

———

Teri checked Jethro's vitals one more time. Stable and improving.

Smith? Not in trouble. Blood pressure still low, but safe.

Done.

She collapsed back against the aft cargo net.

Somewhere along the way, the flight's pair of crew chiefs had bagged the other two bodies.

She was still aboard the helicopter. She always lost track of everything when there was someone to save.

Keying the intercom, she asked the pilots, "Where are we?"

"Just going feet wet. About ten minutes to the ship. What's the count?"

"Two DOA before we touched them. Two stable. One uninjured."

"Other flight saved one of four—another alive, but probably won't make it to the ship. Well done, Medic."

That's when she realized that the Air Force crew

didn't even know her name. "Thanks," she released the intercom and it was back to just her and Doc on the med circuit.

He checked over both patients, then blanketed them up to their necks despite the heat. Not a bad call. He actually blushed as he covered over Smith's chest, which was pretty funny.

She really looked at Doc for the first time. Her family was all sleek and neat. Elegant. Doc looked like he could play football, though he only had an inch or so on her.

"Why are *you* the black sheep?" Teri asked in turn.

Doc sighed. "Army instead of med school. Only one in the family."

"But you *are* a medic."

Doc laughed easily. "No, I'm a grunt. I've had that tag for about an hour—Smith's doing. Guess it's because I know how to unroll gauze without breaking into a nervous sweat."

His movements finally made sense. Instincts trained by growing up in a medical family but no formal training. Yet he'd helped save one. "Is that why you apologized to Smith *before* you tapped her for the IV?"

"Yeah, never done that before. But given enough blood to make a fair guess. Your turn."

"Artist family. I *am* a medic," she found it easy to tease him, a little.

"Baaa!" Doc offered in commiseration that made her feel as if she belonged rather than her usually totally not. "Your 'art' just saved two lives, works for me. Jethro was a damn good man."

"Will still be." He wasn't dead after all.

"I meant he was a damn good man when I was willing to fight beside him."

"And now you're not."

Doc seemed to shrink. "You ever been in a firefight, Teri?"

"Edges. Night Stalkers medics may fly right into the battle to do a rescue, but we've got the best gunners in the business for protection."

"This one was front and center. Seven of nine down hard. Sounds like five dead." He actually shuddered. "Never want to watch or be in charge of something like that again."

"Yet you're, well, you and Smith were the ones who survived. Were good enough to make it."

"Her skill, my luck."

The helo slowed abruptly and settled to the sprawling deck of the *Peleliu* helicopter carrier ship.

The doors slammed open before they were fully settled onto the deck. Corpsmen with stretchers were waiting and in the swirl of unloading she lost track of Doc Carson.

Which was really too bad, he was one of the few people she'd ever been comfortable just talking to.

9

"Tried to check out there, Smith. Damn glad you didn't." Gerrard dropped into the chair beside her bed in the ship's infirmary. "The *Peleliu* might be an old boat, but their docs—real ones, not like me—are top notch. Say you'll be good as new after they stitched up some of the inside stuff."

Smith shrugged, then winced. "Heard you had something to do with that."

Now it was his turn to shrug...and wait.

No thanks. Nothing. *Just the facts, man.*

He took his life in his hands and laughed at her. "You always were a chatty bitch."

At that she offered one of her lethal smiles. "Took out more of them than us; I'm happy."

"You mean you saved our asses. Damn but you can shoot, girl."

A passing Captain stopped and looked down at them. He was one of those tall, square-jawed, poster-soldier types. He wore mirrored Ray Bans even though they were several decks down in the ship.

"You a shooter?" he asked.

"She is. Best damn one I've ever seen," Doc answered for her because Smith was busy squinting at the guy as if she could read something through those mirrored shades.

"You the DAP Hawk pilot?" Smith asked him.

"Best damn one you'll ever see," he said with a straight face. "We've got a need of good gunners. Mechanics, too."

"Can hotwire a car faster than you can crash a helo," Smith snapped back.

Yet another piece of news Doc hadn't known.

"Good start. Work on that. Got a name?" Mr. Shades asked.

"Smith. Kee Smith."

Doc looked over at her. He'd never heard her first name before. Maybe that's why she never got a tag that stuck; Smith didn't give anyone a thing to work with.

"You?" Smith asked the guy in the glasses.

"Yeah, I've got a name." His grin was almost as lethal as Smith's before he twisted on his heel and walked out.

"Who the hell was that asshole?"

Doc had no idea.

"Viper Henderson," Teri said from just behind his shoulder, making him twitch around to look at her. "Captain in command of the Night Stalkers 5D."

With no mask or helmet, and her blonde hair fluttering around her jawline, she looked amazing.

"Huh." Smith made a thoughtful sound. Then she

looked at him. "I'm gonna live, Doc. Get outta here. Go save someone else's life."

He glanced up at Teri who was watching him intently. At a loss for what else to do, he rose to his feet. It never paid to argue with Smith.

Together, he and Teri checked in on Jethro who was awake.

"Don't walk in front of so many bullets next time, Bob."

"Whatever you say, Sarge."

"Bob?" Teri asked.

"Corporal Bob Bodine," Jethro grimaced up at her. "Jethro Bodine from *The Beverly Hillbillies,* Jed Clampett's, uh, challenged nephew. I dropped my dinner tray in the damn chow line once—*once*—and now I guess I'm labeled for life."

"Maybe not. You did good today. Thanks for that last mag. It made a real difference. I'll make damn sure it's in my report." It hadn't actually mattered because of the Night Stalkers' timely arrival, but there was no need for Jethro to know that. "Maybe 'Last Mag' Bodine?"

He smiled, "Kinda like that. We'll see if it sticks. Thanks for saving my ass, Sarge."

"She did all the tricky shit," he hooked a thumb at Teri.

"Yes, but you got me to her still breathing."

Doc and Teri drifted through the ship together. He wasn't sure exactly who was leading who, but he definitely didn't know his way around such a big ship. The *Peleliu* was eight hundred feet of helicopter carrier. Down on the hangar deck, all the way aft, there was a sweeping view of equatorial Atlantic, but still comfortably shaded by the cool steel overhead.

They sat and just stared out at the water together for a long time.

"What you said to him, goes for you too, you know?" Teri's voice was little louder than the low rumble of the ship's engine and the high whine of an impact drill at the far end of the hangar bay. They were doing some kind of service on one of the helos.

"What's that?"

"Well done. You got out alive. You defended your team when it mattered. Gave me a chance to save Jethro by taking care of Smith."

"No way is he ever gonna shed Jethro for 'Last Mag' but I liked giving him a moment of hope."

Her smile agreed. "Still, that was really kind. How about keeping your Doc tag?"

"That's not me. Guess I'm back to 'Low Gear' until I can get out."

"Out?"

He couldn't bring himself to look at her. "Gun battle like that. People dying all around you. Not able to do shit about it except a couple patches of gauze. Isn't some place I want to be going back to anytime soon."

10

Teri noticed the slump of Doc's shoulders but didn't know what to say. Not like she was some wizard counselor or maybe she'd have her own shit together.

"Of course," he muttered to himself, "No idea what the crap I'm good for if I do get out."

"Medic," she said it without thought.

He snorted. "Yeah right."

"I'm serious."

He finally turned to look at her. "I don't see you becoming some amazing painter or photographer."

"Not my skill. It's clear that medical is yours."

"My sister's gonna be a brain surgeon. Mom is a top OR nurse. Dad's the cutter for Boston's biggest ER. How am I supposed to compete with any of that?"

Teri used to ask herself the same question. She had none of the skills. But her desire to fit in the family had made her try—unsuccessfully—for years.

Doc was back to scowling out at the rolling ocean.

"So don't."

"Don't what?"

"Don't compete."

Again he turned to her. Each time he did, it was as if she could see him more clearly. Not disjointed like one of her brother's paintings or, even stranger, Dad's semi-realistic Mexican Day-of-the-Dead imagery as if he weren't Scottish.

"Don't compete. You have the makings of being a damn fine medic. How many would never have made it out of that hole at all without your help? Jethro would never have made it alive to my bird. Probably not Smith either. You've got the right instincts, the right level of care, and I didn't see you doing any of the normal squeams about doing the hard stuff. Just like Viper told Smith they need gunners, our Combat Search-and-Rescue team needs trained medics. Good ones, who know how important it is that we fly right into a battle zone if it means saving people."

His smile went sideways, which meant something had struck him funny.

"What?"

"That's an awful lot of words for Teri Carson of the Alaskan Carsons."

"Sue me."

He laughed, but this time the smile was all for her. "Medic, huh?"

But he wasn't doing the staring out at the ocean while he thought. He was looking right at her.

All she could do was nod.

"How long to train up?"

"Depends on your instructor and how hard you're

willing to work. Three months to active duty. Nine months to lead. A couple years to do the kind of things I just did for Jethro."

This time his gaze shifted to thoughtful. "I actually like the sound of that. Saving Jethro and Smith felt good. I could like that a lot. Know any good instructors?"

"I do."

The question was, did she want to take on someone like Doc as a student? Maybe as more than a student?

"I know a damn good one." It seemed that she did.

When he caught her meaning, that smile went ever so bright. Like he was tasting sunshine.

He raised his hand, facing her. "Go Team Black Sheep!"

That she high-fived him for.

He spread his fingers and she let her own interlace with his.

Yes, it *was* just like sunshine.

DANIEL'S CHRISTMAS
(EXCERPT)

IF YOU LIKED THIS, YOU'LL LOVE THE
NIGHT STALKERS WHITE HOUSE NOVELS!

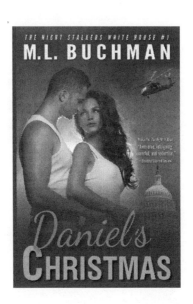

DANIEL'S CHRISTMAS

(EXCERPT)

The phone hammered him awake. Daniel came to in his office chair with the phone already to his ear.

Someone was speaking rapidly. He caught perhaps one word in three. "CIA. Immediate briefing. North Korea."

He must have made some intelligible reply as moments later he was listening to a dial tone.

Daniel rubbed at his eyes, but the vista didn't change. Large cherry wood desk. Mounds of work in neatly stacked folders that he'd sat down to tackle after the long flight. His briefcase still unopened on the floor beside him. Definitely the White House Chief of Staff's office. His office. Nightmare or reality? Both. Definitely.

Phone. He'd been on the phone.

The words came back and, now fully awake, Daniel started swearing even as he grabbed the handset and began dialing.

Maybe he could blame all this on Emily Beale. In the three short weeks she'd been at the White House, Daniel had risen from being the First Lady's secretary to the White House Chief of Staff and it was partly Emily's fault. As if his life had been battered by a tornado. Still felt that way a year later.

Okay, call it mostly her fault.

As he listened to the phone ringing in his ear, it felt better to have someone to blame. He rubbed at his eyes. A year later and he still didn't know whether to curse Major Beale or thank her.

Maybe he could make it all her fault.

"Yagumph."

"Good morning, Mr. President."

"Is it morning?" The deep voice would have been incomprehensibly groggy without the familiarity of long practice.

Daniel checked his watch, barely morning. "Yes, sir!" he offered his most chipper voice.

"Crap! What? All of 12:03?"

"12:10, sir." They'd been on the ground just over an hour.

"Double crap!" The President was slowly gaining in clarity, maybe one in ten linguists would be able to understand him now.

"Seven more minutes of sleep than you guessed, sir."

"Daniel?"

"Yes, Mr. President?"

"Next time Major Beale comes to town, I'm sending you up on one of her training rides."

"Sounds like fun, sir." If he had a death wish. "Crashing in the Lincoln Memorial Reflecting Pool is definitely an experience I can't wait to relive." The Major was also the childhood friend of the President, so he had to walk with a little care, but not much. The two of them were that close.

"Time to get up, sir, the CIA is coming calling. They'll be here in twenty minutes."

"I'll be there in ten." A low groan sounded over the phone. "Make that fifteen." The handset rattled loudly as he missed the cradle. Daniel got the phone clear of his ear before the President's handset dropped on the floor.

Daniel hung up and considered sleeping for the another fifteen minutes. There was a nice sofa along the far wall sitting in a close group with a couple of armchairs, but he'd have to stand up to reach it. All in strong, dusky red leather, his secretary's doing after discovering Daniel had no taste. Janet had also ordered in a beautiful oriental rug and several large framed photographs. Even on the first day she'd known him well enough to chose images of wide-open spaces. He missed his family farm, but the photos helped him when D.C. was squeezing in too hard.

If he didn't stand and resisted the urge to seek more sleep, all that remained was to consider his desk. Its elegant cherry wood surface lost beneath a sea of reports and files.

Fifteen minutes. He could read the briefing paper on Chinese coal, review tomorrow's agenda which, if he were lucky, might stay on schedule for at least the first quarter hour of a planned fourteen-hour day. Or he could just order up a giant burn bag and be done with the whole mess.

He picked up whatever was on top of the nearest stack.

An Advent calendar.

Janet, had to be.

Well, the woman had taste. It was beautiful; encased in a soft, tooled-leather portfolio and tied closed with a narrow red ribbon done up in a neat bow. He pulled a loose end and opened the calendar. Inside were three spreads of stunning hand-painted pictures on deep-set pages. He took a moment to admire the first one.

It was a depiction of Santa and his reindeer. Except Santa might have been a particularly pudgy hamster and the reindeer might have been mice with improbable antlers. One might have had a red nose, or he might have had his eggnog spiked; the artist had left that open to interpretation. A couple of rabbits were helping to load the sleigh. Little numbered doors were set in the side of the sleigh, as well as in a nearby tree, and in the snow at the micedeer's paws. The page was thick enough that a small treat could be hidden behind each little door.

He shook the calendar lightly and heard things rattling. Probably little sweets and tidbits to hit his notorious sweet tooth.

The day Janet retired he'd be in so much trouble. Not only did she manage to keep his life organized, she also managed to make him smile, even when things were coming apart at the seams. Midnight calls from the CIA for immediate meetings didn't bode well, yet here he was dangerously close to enjoying the moment.

He started to open the little door with a tiny golden number "1" on the green ribbon pull tab. The door depicted a candy-cane colored present perched high on the sleigh.

"Don't do that."

He looked up.

A woman stood in the doorway, closely escorted by one of the service Marines. A short wave of russet hair curled partly over her face and trickled down just far enough to emphasize the line of her neck. Her bangs ruffled in a gentle wave covering one eye. The eye in the clear shone a striking hazel against pale skin. She wore a thick, woolen cardigan, a bit darker than her hair, open at the front over an electric blue turtleneck that appeared to say, "Joy to the World." At least based on the letters he could see.

"Don't do what?"

"Don't open it early," she nodded toward the calendar in his hands. "That's cheating."

He double-checked his watch. "It's twelve-eighteen on December first. That's not cheating."

"Not until nighttime, after sunset. That's what Mama always said."

"And your Mama is always right?"

"Damn straight." Though her expression momentarily belied her cheerful insistence.

He glanced at the Marine. "Kenneth. Does she have a purpose here?"

She sauntered into his office as if it were her own living room and an armed Marine was not following two paces behind her. More guts than most, or a complete unawareness of how close she was to being wrestled to the ground by a member of the U.S. Military.

"Remember what they say about the book and the cover?"

"Sure, don't judge." He inspected her wrinkled black corduroys and did his best not to appreciate the nice line they made of her legs.

She dropped into one of the leather chairs in front of his desk and propped a pair of alarmingly green sneakers with red laces on the cherry wood. At least they were clean. All she'd need to complete the image would be to pop a bright pink gum bubble at him. And maybe some of those foam slip-on reindeer antlers. He offered her a smile as she slouched lower in the chair. In turn, she offered him a clear view most of the way to her tonsils with a massive yawn.

She managed to cover it before it was completely done.

"Sorry, I've been up for three days researching this. Director Smith said I should bring it right over." She waved a slim portfolio at him that he hadn't previously noticed.

CIA Director Smith. Well, that explained who she was. Whatever lay in that portfolio was the reason he'd only had forty-five minutes of sleep so far tonight. And he'd spent that slumped in his chair. He did his best to surreptitiously straighten his jacket and tie.

"You've been researching." Maybe a prompt would get her to the point more quickly.

"Yes, Mr. Darlington. I'm Dr. Alice Thompson, with dual masters in Afghani and Mathematics at Columbia. Which makes me a dueling master. PhD in digital imaging at NYU and an analyst for the CIA. Which means something, but I have no idea what. The reason you're awake right now is to meet with me."

"No, the reason I'm awake right now is to meet with both you and the President."

"The President?" She jerked upright in her chair, her feet dropping to the floor. "No one said anything about that to me."

ABOUT THE AUTHOR

USA Today and Amazon #1 Bestseller M. L. "Matt" Buchman started writing on a flight south from Japan to ride his bicycle across the Australian Outback. Just part of a solo around-the-world trip that ultimately launched his writing career.

From the very beginning, his powerful female heroines insisted on putting character first, *then* a great adventure. He's since written over 60 action-adventure thrillers and military romantic suspense novels. And just for the fun of it: 100 short stories, and a fast-growing pile of read-by-author audiobooks.

Booklist says: "3X Top 10 of the Year." PW says: "Tom Clancy fans open to a strong female lead will clamor for more." His fans say: "I want more now...of everything." That his characters are even more insistent than his fans is a hoot.

As a 30-year project manager with a geophysics degree who has designed and built houses, flown and jumped out of planes, and solo-sailed a 50' ketch, he is awed by what is possible. More at: www.mlbuchman.com.

Other works by M. L. Buchman: *(* - also in audio)*

Other works by M. L. Buchman:

Contemporary Romance (cont)

Where Dreams
Where Dreams are Born
Where Dreams Reside
Where Dreams Are of Christmas
Where Dreams Unfold
Where Dreams Are Written

Science Fiction / Fantasy

Deities Anonymous
Cookbook from Hell: Reheated
Saviors 101

Single Titles
The Nara Reaction
Monk's Maze
the Me and Elsie Chronicles

Non-Fiction

Strategies for Success
Managing Your Inner Artist/Writer
Estate Planning for Authors
Character Voice

Short Story Series by M. L. Buchman:

Romantic Suspense

Delta Force
Delta Force

Firehawks
The Firehawks Lookouts
The Firehawks Hotshots
The Firebirds

The Night Stalkers
The Night Stalkers
The Night Stalkers 5E
The Night Stalkers CSAR
The Night Stalkers Wedding Stories

US Coast Guard
US Coast Guard

White House Protection Force
White House Protection Force

Contemporary Romance

Eagle Cove
Eagle Cove

Henderson's Ranch
Henderson's Ranch

Where Dreams
Where Dreams

Thrillers

Dead Chef
Dead Chef

Science Fiction / Fantasy

Deities Anonymous
Deities Anonymous

Other
The Future Night Stalkers
Single Titles

SIGN UP FOR M. L. BUCHMAN'S NEWSLETTER TODAY

and receive:
Release News
Free Short Stories
a Free Book

Get your free book today. Do it now.
free-book.mlbuchman.com

Made in the USA
Columbia, SC
24 May 2020